Here's what kids have to say to
Mary Pope Osborne, author of
the Magic Tree House series:

When I read those books, I feel like I'm in a different world where I could be what I want to be and do what I want to do and go where I want to go.—Ross E.

Out of the 3,000 books I've read, your books are the best.—Lauren S.

I love your books so much that I could read them with my eyes closed.—Gabriel R.

I normally like to watch TV, so my mom likes it when she sees me reading your books. Please write some more.—Brian B.

I love your books. I feel like I am Jack and Annie. I like reading like Jack. I like pretending like Annie.—Robin P.

Your books are so educational.—Allan D.

I don't like reading. But your stories are so interesting that I love reading them.—Katy P.

I wish I could spend my life reading the Magic Tree House series.—Juliette S.

Parents and teachers love
Magic Tree House books, too!

[After reading Pirates Past Noon*], I
realized we were "in the middle" of the
series, so I ordered all the other books...
I wish you could have seen my children's
reactions to seeing the other books. It does a
teacher's heart good to see children "fighting
over books"!*—D. Bowers

*I thank you for your wonderful contribution
to children's literature—and to my classroom
as well.*—E. Mellinger

*Your series is named correctly, having the
word* magic *in the title. They truly are
magical books.*—J. Royer

Dear Readers,

I have long wanted to send Jack and Annie to China, but I couldn't figure out what period of history they should visit. Then one day, when I was reading in my local library, I stumbled across some amazing information. In the 1970s, archaeologists began excavating a great wonder in China: an ancient burial tomb with over 7,000 statues of soldiers and horses. The tomb was more than 2,000 years old and had been built for the first Chinese emperor.

After I learned this, I found other library books about that period of Chinese history, and I spent days reading and taking notes. From these notes, I fashioned <u>Day of the Dragon King.</u>

Have I told you before that libraries are very important to me? They are <u>my</u> magic places...where I dream and wonder...and spin my stories.

Visit <u>your</u> library and I bet you'll find the same magic!

All my best,

Mary Pope Osborne

Day of the Dragon King

by Mary Pope Osborne

illustrated by Sal Murdocca

A STEPPING STONE BOOK™

Random House 🏠 New York

For Peter and Andrew Boyce

Text copyright © 1998 by Mary Pope Osborne
Illustrations copyright © 1998 by Sal Murdocca
All rights reserved under International and Pan-American Copyright Conventions.
Published in the United States by Random House, Inc., New York, and
simultaneously in Canada by Random House of Canada Limited, Toronto.

www.randomhouse.com/magictreehouse/

Library of Congress Cataloging-in-Publication Data
Osborne, Mary Pope.
Day of the Dragon King / by Mary Pope Osborne ; illustrated by Sal Murdocca.
    p.   cm. — (Magic tree house ; #14)   "Stepping Stone book."
Summary: The magic treehouse takes Jack and Annie back two thousand years to
ancient China where they must find the original copy of an old legend before the
Imperial Library is burned down by the evil Dragon King.
ISBN 0-679-89051-3 (pbk.) — ISBN 0-679-99051-8 (lib. bdg.)
[1. Time travel—Fiction.   2. China—History—Han dynasty, 202 B.C.–220 A.D.—
Fiction.   3. Magic—Fiction.   4. Tree houses—Fiction.]   I. Murdocca, Sal, ill.   II.
Title.   III. Series: Osborne, Mary Pope. Magic tree house series ; #14.
PZ7.O81167Day   1998   [Fic]—dc21   97-49199

Printed in the United States of America   50 49 48 47 46 45 44 43

Random House, Inc. New York, Toronto, London, Sydney, Auckland
A STEPPING STONE BOOK is a trademark of Random House, Inc.

Contents

Prologue

One summer day in Frog Creek, Pennsylvania, a mysterious tree house appeared in the woods.

Eight-year-old Jack and his seven-year-old sister, Annie, climbed into the tree house. They found that it was filled with books.

Jack and Annie soon discovered that the tree house was magic. It could take them to the places in the books. All they had to do was point to a picture and wish to go there.

Along the way, they discovered that the

tree house belongs to Morgan le Fay. Morgan is a magical librarian from the time of King Arthur. She travels through time and space, gathering books.

In Magic Tree House #12, *Polar Bears Past Bedtime*, Jack and Annie solved the last of four ancient riddles and became Master Librarians. To help them in their future tasks, Morgan gave Jack and Annie secret library cards with the letters <u>M L</u> on them.

Jack and Annie's first four missions as Master Librarians are to save stories from ancient libraries. When their first adventure ended (Magic Tree House #13, *Vacation Under the Volcano*), Morgan asked them to return to the tree house in two weeks to go to China and save another story.

Now the two weeks are over…

Day of the
Dragon King

1

The Bamboo Book

Annie peeked into Jack's room.

"Ready to go to China?" she asked.

Jack took a deep breath.

"Sure," he answered.

"Bring your secret library card," Annie said. "I have mine in my pocket."

"Yep," said Jack.

He opened his top dresser drawer and took out a thin wooden card. The letters M L on it shimmered in the light. Jack dropped the card into his backpack. Then he threw in his notebook and a pencil.

"Let's go," said Annie.

Jack pulled on his pack and followed her.

What are we in for today? he wondered.

"Bye, Mom!" said Annie as they passed their mom in the kitchen.

"Where are you going?" she asked.

"China!" said Annie.

"Great," said their mom. She winked at them. "Have fun."

Fun? thought Jack. He was afraid that *fun* wasn't quite the right word.

"Just wish us luck," he said as he and Annie headed out the front door.

"Good luck!" their mother called.

"If only she knew we aren't pretending," Jack whispered to Annie.

"Yeah," said Annie, grinning.

Outside, the sun shone brightly. Birds sang. Crickets chirped. Jack and Annie walked up their street toward the Frog Creek woods.

"I wonder if the weather will be this nice in China," Annie said.

"I don't know. Remember, Morgan said this would be a very scary adventure," said Jack.

"They're always scary," said Annie. "But we always meet animals who help us, or people."

"True," said Jack.

"I bet we meet someone *great* today," said Annie.

Jack smiled. He was starting to feel excited now instead of scared.

"Let's hurry!" he said.

They ran into the Frog Creek woods. They slipped between the tall trees until they came to a huge oak.

"Hello!" came a soft voice they knew well.

They looked up. Morgan was peering down from the magic tree house.

"Ready for your next mission as Master Librarians?" she asked.

"Yes!" said Jack and Annie.

They grabbed the rope ladder and started up.

"Are we still going to China?" asked Annie when they had climbed into the tree house.

"Indeed," said Morgan. "You're going to *ancient* China. Here is the title of the story you must find."

She held up a long, thin strip of wood. It

looked like a ruler, except it had strange writing on it instead of numbers.

"Long ago, the Chinese discovered how to make paper. It was one of the world's most important discoveries," said Morgan. "But you are going to a time earlier than that, to a time when books were written on bamboo strips like this one."

"Wow," said Annie, pointing at the figures on the bamboo. "So *this* is Chinese writing?"

"Yes," said Morgan. "Just as we have letters, Chinese writing is made up of many characters. Each one stands for a different thing or idea. These characters are the title of an ancient Chinese legend. You must find the first writing of the legend before the Imperial Library is destroyed."

"Hurry, let's go," said Annie.

"Wait, we need our research book," said Jack.

"Yes, you do," said Morgan.

From the folds of her robe, she pulled out a book. On the cover was the title: *The Time of the First Emperor.*

Morgan handed the book to Jack.

"This research book will *guide* you," she said. "But remember, in your darkest hour, only the old legend can *save* you."

"But we have to find it first," said Annie.

"Exactly," said Morgan.

She handed Jack the bamboo strip, and he slipped it into his pack.

Jack pushed his glasses into place, then pointed at the cover of their research book.

"I wish we could go there!" he said.

The wind started to blow.

The tree house started to spin. It spun faster and faster.

Then everything was still.

Absolutely still.

2

The Cowherd

"Oh, wow," Annie said. "These clothes feel so soft. And look, I have a pocket for my secret library card."

Jack opened his eyes. Their clothes had magically changed.

They no longer wore jeans, T-shirts, and sneakers. Instead, they had on baggy pants, loose shirts, straw shoes, and round hats. Annie's shirt had a pocket in it.

Jack saw that his backpack had become a

rough cloth sack. Inside were his research book, his notebook, his library card, and the bamboo strip.

"Cows," said Annie, looking out the window.

Jack looked out, too. The tree house had landed in a lone tree in a sunny field. Cows grazed, and a young man stood watching over them. At the edge of the field was a farmhouse. Beyond the house was a walled city.

"It looks so peaceful," said Annie.

"You can never be sure," said Jack. "Remember, Pompeii looked peaceful before the volcano went off."

"Oh, yeah," said Annie.

"Let's see what the book says," said Jack.

He reached in the sack and pulled out the China book. He opened it and read aloud:

Over 2,000 years ago, China was ruled by its first emperor. Because he chose the dragon to be his symbol, he was called the "Dragon King." In China, dragons are seen as brave and powerful creatures.

"Dragon King? That sounds a little scary," said Jack.

"I like his outfit," said Annie.

Next to the writing was a picture. It showed a man wearing a rich, flowing robe with wide sleeves. He also wore a tall hat with beads hanging from it.

Jack pulled out his notebook and wrote:

first emperor called Dragon King

"The book we need must be in the Dragon King's library," said Annie. "I bet his palace is in that city."

Jack looked up.

"Right," he said. "And that's how to get there." He pointed across the field to a dirt road that led to the walled city.

"Good plan," said Annie.

She climbed out of the tree house and started down the rope ladder.

Jack threw the China book and his notebook into his sack. He slung the sack over his shoulder and followed Annie.

When they reached the ground, they started through the field.

"Look, that guy's waving at us," said Annie.

The man tending the cows was shouting and waving. He started running toward them.

"Uh-oh, what's he want?" said Jack.

A moment later, the man stood in their path. He was young and handsome with a kind face.

"Can you do me a great favor?" he asked. "I would be most grateful."

"Of course," said Annie.

"Give a message to the silk weaver. You will see her at the farmhouse," said the young man. "Tell her to meet me here at twilight."

"Sure, no problem," said Annie.

The young man smiled.

"Thank you," he said. Then he started to leave.

"Wait, excuse me—" said Jack. "Do you know where we can find the Imperial Library?"

A look of horror crossed the man's kind face.

"Why?" he whispered.

"Oh, I—I just wondered," said Jack.

The young man shook his head.

"Beware of the Dragon King," he said. "Whatever you do, *beware*."

Then he turned and ran back to his cows.

"Oh, man," whispered Jack. "Now we know one thing for sure."

"What?" asked Annie.

"This place is *not* as peaceful as it seems," Jack said.

3

The Silk Weaver

Jack and Annie kept walking across the pasture toward the road. Annie stopped when they neared the farmhouse.

"We have to find the silk weaver and give her the message," she said.

"Let's do that on our way back," said Jack. "I'm worried about finding the Imperial Library."

"What if we don't have time?" said Annie. "We promised. And he was so nice."

Jack sighed.

"Okay," he said. "But let's find her fast. And remember to keep your head down so no one will notice us."

Jack and Annie bowed their heads as they headed toward the house.

As they got closer, Jack peeked out from under his hat. An ox pulled a cart filled with hay. Men hoed the ground. Women pushed wheelbarrows piled high with grain.

"There!" said Annie. She pointed to an open porch where a young woman was weaving cloth on a loom. "That must be her!"

Annie ran to the silk weaver. Jack looked around to see if anyone was watching. Luckily, all the farmworkers seemed too busy to notice anything. Still looking around carefully, Jack walked toward the porch.

Annie was already talking to the silk weaver.

"What did he say?" the young woman asked. Her voice was soft but strong. Her dark eyes glowed with happiness.

"He said you should meet him in the field at twilight," said Annie. "He's so handsome!"

"Yes, he is." The silk weaver gave Annie a shy smile. Then she reached down to a basket near her loom and picked up a ball of yellow thread.

"It was very brave of you to bring the message," she said. "Please accept this silk thread as my thank-you."

She handed Annie the ball of silk.

"It's beautiful," said Annie. "Feel."

She handed it to Jack. The thread was smooth and soft.

"How do you make silk?" said Jack.

"It is made from the cocoons of silk-worms," said the weaver.

"Really? Worms? That's neat," said Jack. "Let me write that down."

He reached into his sack.

"Please don't!" said the silk weaver. "The making of silk is China's most valuable secret. Anyone who steals the secret will be arrested. The Dragon King will have him put to death."

"Oops," said Jack.

He dropped the ball of silk into his sack.

"I think you must leave quickly," whispered the silk weaver. "You have been seen."

Jack looked over his shoulder. A man was pointing at them.

"Let's go," he said.

"Bye!" said Annie. "Good luck on your date!"

"Thank you," the silk weaver said.

"Come on," said Jack.

They hurried away from the silk weaver.

"Stop!" someone shouted.

"Run!" said Annie.

4

The Great Wall

Jack and Annie ran around the farmhouse. At the back was an oxcart filled with bags of grain. There was no one in sight.

The shouting behind them got louder.

Jack and Annie looked at each other, then dived into the back of the wooden cart. They buried themselves in the middle of the bags of grain.

Jack's heart pounded as the shouts came closer. He held his breath and waited for the people to leave.

Suddenly the cart lurched forward. Some-one was driving them away!

Jack and Annie peeked over the bags. Jack saw the back of the driver. He was calm-ly steering the oxcart over the dirt road. They were on their way to the walled city!

Jack and Annie ducked down again.

"This is great!" whispered Annie. "All we have to do is jump out when we get into the city."

"Yep," Jack said softly. "Then we'll find the Imperial Library, find the book, and get back to the magic tree house."

"No problem," whispered Annie.

"Whoa!" The cart slowly came to a halt.

Jack held his breath. He heard voices and the heavy tramping of feet—lots of feet. He and Annie peeked out.

"Oh, man," he whispered.

A long line of men was crossing the road in front of the cart. They carried axes, shovels, and hoes. Guards marched alongside them.

"Let's find out what's happening," said Jack.

He reached into his sack and pulled out the China book. Pushing his glasses into place, he found a picture of the workers. He read:

The Dragon King forced many of his subjects to start building a wall to protect China from invaders. Later emperors made the wall even longer. Finally, it stretched 3,700 miles along China's border. The Great Wall of China is the longest structure ever built.

"Wow, the Great Wall of China," said Jack.

"I've heard of that," said Annie.

"Who hasn't?" said Jack. "Those guys are going to work on it right now."

Just then, someone grabbed Jack and Annie. They looked up. It was the driver of the cart.

"Who are you?" he asked angrily.

"We—uh—" Jack didn't know what to say.

The man's gaze fell on the open book in Jack's hands. His mouth dropped open. He let go of Jack and Annie. Slowly he reached out and touched the book. He looked back at Jack and Annie with wide eyes.

"What is *this?*" he said.

5

The Scholar

"It's a book from our country," said Jack. "Your books are made of bamboo, but ours are made of paper. Actually, *your* country invented paper. But later, in the future."

The man looked confused.

"Never mind," said Annie. "It's for reading. It's for learning about faraway places."

The man stared at them. Tears filled his eyes.

"What's wrong?" Annie asked softly.

"I *love* reading and learning," he said.

"So do I," said Jack.

The man smiled. "You don't understand! I am dressed as a farmer," he said. "But in truth, I am a scholar!"

"What's a *scholar?*" said Annie.

"We are great readers, learners, and writers," he said. "We have long been the most honored citizens in China."

The scholar's smile faded.

"But now scholars are in danger," he said. "And many of us have gone into hiding."

"Why?" said Jack.

"The Dragon King is afraid of the power of our books and learning," said the scholar. "He wants people to think only what he wants them to think. Any day he may order *the burning of the books!*"

28

Annie gasped.

"Does that mean what I think it means?" said Jack.

The scholar nodded.

"All the books in the Imperial Library will be burned," he said.

"That's rotten!" said Annie.

"Indeed it is!" the scholar said quietly.

"Listen, we have a mission to get a book from that library," said Jack.

"Who are you?" asked the scholar.

"Show him," said Annie.

She reached into her shirt pocket as Jack reached into his sack. They brought out the secret library cards. The letters shimmered in the sunlight.

The scholar's mouth dropped open again.

"You are Master Librarians," he said. "I

have never met ones so honored who were so young."

He bowed to show his respect.

"Thank you," said Jack and Annie.

They bowed back to him.

"How can I help you?" asked the scholar.

"We need to go to the Imperial Library and find this book," said Jack.

He held out Morgan's bamboo strip to the scholar.

"We will go to the Imperial Library," said the scholar. "As for the story, I know it well. It is a true one, written not long ago. But I warn you. We will be in great danger."

"We know!" said Annie.

The scholar smiled.

"I am happy to be doing something I believe in again," said the scholar. "Let us go!"

They all climbed into the front of the cart. The long line of wall builders was marching in the distance. As the oxen started forward, the scholar turned to Jack and Annie.

"Where are you from?" he asked.

"Frog Creek, Pennsylvania," said Annie.

"I have never heard of it," said the scholar. "Do they have a library there?"

"Oh, sure, there's a library in every town," said Jack. "In fact, there are probably thousands of libraries in our country."

"And millions of books," said Annie. "And no one burns them."

"Right," said Jack. "Everyone gets to go to school to learn to read them."

The scholar stared at him and shook his head.

"It sounds like paradise," he said.

6

The Dragon King

The oxcart bumped across the wooden bridge that crossed over a moat. Then it passed guards standing by giant wooden gates.

"Are the gates ever closed?" Jack asked.

"Oh, yes, every day at sunset," said the scholar. "When the gong sounds, the gates close. The bridge comes up. And the city is sealed shut for the night."

"I guess visitors have to leave before that happens," Annie said. "Or they'll be stuck here for the whole night. Right?"

"Yes," said the scholar.

The cart bumped between the city gates.

Rows of small houses were bunched together on either side of the street. They were made of mud with straw roofs. People cooked over outdoor fires. They washed their clothes in wooden tubs.

As the oxcart bumped along, the houses got larger. These were made of painted wood and pottery tiles. They all had curved roofs.

"Why are those roofs like that?" asked Jack.

"To keep away the bad spirits," said the scholar.

"How do they do that?" said Annie.

"The spirits can only travel in straight lines," said the scholar.

"Wow," whispered Annie.

The cart went by some open tea shops. Then it passed a large market square filled with stalls and shoppers. People were buying and selling fish, chickens, firewood, wagon wheels, silk cloth, furs, and jade jewelry.

Some people were lined up at a stall filled with tiny cages.

"What's for sale there?" said Annie.

"Crickets," the scholar said. "They make good pets. You can feed them tea leaves and enjoy their delicate song."

The cart moved on toward the Dragon King's walled palace. They stopped in front of the palace gates.

"Grain delivery!" the scholar shouted up to the guard at the tower.

The guard waved them through. Inside were beautiful gardens and huge mounds of earth surrounded by a low brick wall.

"That is the Imperial Burial Grounds," said the scholar, pointing at the mounds.

"Who is buried there?" asked Jack.

"The ancestors of the Dragon King," said the scholar.

"What are *ancestors?*" Annie asked.

"They are the people in your family who lived before you," said the scholar. "Someday the Dragon King himself will be buried there. Three hundred thousand workers have been building his burial tomb."

"Oh, man," said Jack.

He looked over his shoulder at the burial grounds. He wondered why it took so many workers to build a tomb.

"*No!*" said the scholar.

Jack whirled around.

"What's wrong?" he asked.

The scholar pointed at the palace courtyard. A dark cloud of smoke was rising into the sky.

"*Fire!*" said the scholar.

"*The books!*" said Jack.

"*Hurry!*" said Annie.

The scholar snapped the reins. The oxen trotted up the stone path. When the cart rolled into the courtyard, soldiers were everywhere.

Some threw wood on a huge bonfire. Others were carrying bamboo strips down the steep stairs that led from the palace.

"Are those books?" asked Jack.

"Yes. The strips are tied together into different bundles," moaned the scholar. "Each bundle is a book."

"Look!" said Annie, pointing to the palace entrance.

Stepping outside was a man in a rich, flowing robe and a tall hat. Jack knew him at once—*the Dragon King!*

7

The Burning of the Books

The Dragon King watched the bonfire as it blazed up toward the sky. Around the fire the air was thick and wavy. Bamboo books were stacked beside the fire, waiting to be burned.

"Hurry!" said the scholar.

They jumped down from the cart and joined the crowd by the bonfire.

The Dragon King shouted to the soldiers. They began throwing the books into the fire. The bamboo crackled as it burned.

"Stop!" cried Annie.

Jack grabbed her.

"Quiet!" he said.

Annie pulled away.

"Stop!" she shouted again. But her voice was lost in the noise of the roaring fire.

"*There's* your story!" said the scholar.

He pointed to a bamboo book that had fallen off a waiting stack.

"I'll get it!" said Annie.

She dashed over to the book.

"Annie!" cried Jack.

But she had already snatched up the bundle of bamboo strips and was charging back to them.

"Got it! Quick, put it in your sack!" she said.

Jack put the bundle of bamboo strips in his

sack. Then he looked around fearfully. He gasped.

The Dragon King was glaring at them! Then he headed their way.

"Seize them!" the Dragon King shouted.

"Run through the burial grounds!" the scholar said to Jack and Annie. "The soldiers will be afraid to follow. They fear the spirits of the ancestors!"

"Thanks!" said Jack. "Thanks for everything!"

"Good luck!" cried Annie.

Then she and Jack took off. Soldiers shouted after them. An arrow whizzed by.

But Jack and Annie kept running. They ran down the path to the burial grounds. They jumped over the low brick wall and ran between the huge mounds of earth.

Suddenly arrows filled the air around them. The archers were shooting from the tower!

"Look!" cried Jack.

There was a doorway in one of the mounds. Jack and Annie ducked inside.

They were in a long hall lit with oil lamps.

"It's so quiet," said Annie. She walked down the passageway. "Hey, there are some steps here."

"Don't go any farther!" said Jack.

"Why not?" said Annie.

"We don't know what's down there," said Jack. "This is a burial tomb, remember? It's creepy."

"Let's just take a quick look," said Annie. "Maybe it's the way out of here."

Jack took a deep breath.

"You might be right," he said. "Okay, but go slow." He didn't want to stumble upon a dead body.

Annie started down the steep steps. Jack followed. The lamps lit their way as they kept going down and down. Finally, they reached the bottom.

Jack blinked. Even though oil lamps glowed everywhere, it was hard to see at first.

When Jack's eyes got used to the strange light, his heart nearly stopped.

"Oh, man," he breathed.

They were in a room *filled* with soldiers— thousands of them.

8

The Tomb

Jack and Annie stood frozen.

The silent soldiers did, too.

Finally, Annie spoke.

"They're fake," she said.

"Fake?" whispered Jack.

"They're not real," she said.

"They *look* real," said Jack.

Annie walked straight toward the front row of soldiers.

Jack held his breath.

Annie pulled the soldier's nose.

"Fake!" she said.

"Oh, brother," said Jack. He walked over to the soldier and touched his painted face. It was as hard as stone.

"It's amazing," Jack said.

Annie nodded. "It's like a museum."

She walked down a row between two lines of soldiers.

"Wait. This is spooky," said Jack. "What *is* this place?"

He put down his sack and pulled out the China book. He found a picture of the frozen army and read aloud:

> **The Dragon King had 7,000 life-size clay figures made for his burial tomb. The clay was baked and painted.**

The Dragon King hoped that the clay army would protect him after he died.

"It's like the pyramid in ancient Egypt," said Jack. "Remember? The queen was buried with a boat and lots of things to take to the afterlife." He looked around. "Annie?"

"I'm here," she called. She was far down another row.

"Come back here," yelled Jack.

"No, *you* come here," said Annie. "It's so cool. All their faces are different."

Jack threw the book into his sack. Then he hurried down the row to Annie.

"Look," she said. "Just look."

In the flickering lamplight, they wandered down the rows of soldiers. No two soldiers had the same nose, the same eyes, or the same mouth.

"Oh, man. No wonder so many people had to work on this tomb," said Jack.

"They really did a good job," said Annie.

"Yeah," said Jack.

There were kneeling archers and foot soldiers dressed in red and black armor.

There were real bronze swords, daggers, axes, spears, bows, and arrows.

There were even life-size wooden chariots with horses. The horses looked completely real. They were different colors with white teeth and red tongues.

"I have to take some notes about all this," said Jack.

He pulled out his notebook and pencil. Then, kneeling on the brick floor, he wrote:

*no two faces the same
not even the horses*

"Ja-ack," said Annie. "You know what?"

"What?"

"I think we're lost," she said.

"Lost?" Jack stood up. "We're not lost."

"Yeah? Then which way is out?" said Annie.

Jack looked around. All he could see were rows of soldiers. In front of them, to the right, to the left, behind them—nothing but clay soldiers.

"Which way did we come?" said Annie.

"I don't know," said Jack.

All the rows looked the same. They stretched out endlessly.

Jack tried not to panic.

"I'd better look this up," he said.

"Forget it," said Annie. "Morgan said the research book would *guide* us. But in our darkest hour, only the ancient legend would *save* us."

"Is this our darkest hour?" asked Jack.

Annie nodded. "Yeah, it's pretty dark."

It does seem to be getting darker in here, thought Jack. The air was getting thicker, too. It seemed harder to breathe.

"Let's ask for help," said Jack.

He reached into the sack and pulled out the bamboo book. He held it up and said,

"Save us!"

As Jack waited, the tomb seemed unbearably quiet.

Jack held the book up again. "Please help us find our way out," he said.

He and Annie kept waiting. But nothing happened.

The air was growing even thicker. The light was getting dimmer. The countless rows of soldiers seemed creepier.

Help did not come.

Jack felt faint. "I—I guess we'll just have—have to—"

"Look!" Annie said.

"What?"

"The ball of thread! It rolled out of your sack!" she said.

"So what?" said Jack.

He looked at his cloth sack lying on the floor. The ball of yellow silk thread *had* rolled out. And it was *still* rolling, leaving a trail of yellow thread!

9

The Silk Path

"What's going on?" said Jack.

"I don't know," said Annie. "But we'd better follow it."

She hurried after the ball of silk thread.

Jack put the bamboo book into his sack and took off after her.

They followed the trail of thread down the row, where it turned down *another* row.

"Hey, that's impossible!" said Jack. "That's scientifically impossible!"

"I told you, it's magic!" cried Annie.

Jack couldn't believe it. But he kept following the thread.

Suddenly the trail of thread was gone. The ball had completely unrolled.

Jack and Annie stood still for a moment and caught their breath.

"What—what now?" said Jack.

"I guess we go up those stairs," Annie said.

"What stairs?" said Jack.

"There."

Jack looked through the dim light and saw the entrance to a stairway only a few feet away.

"Let's get out of here!" he said.

They ran up the stairs. At the top, they saw that they were in the hall that led to the entrance of the mound.

They walked and walked and walked down the lamp-lit passage. Finally, Jack stopped.

"I don't remember this hall being so long," he said.

"Me neither," said Annie. "I guess those weren't the same stairs that we went down."

"What should we do now?" said Jack.

"We'd better keep going," said Annie.

"Yeah, we don't have much choice," said Jack.

They started walking again. They rounded a corner and came to a door.

"Oh, great!" said Annie.

"Wait. We don't know what's on the other side," said Jack. "Go slow. Be careful."

"Okay," said Annie.

Slowly and carefully, she opened the door.

Then she peeked out.

"Yippee," she said softly.

Annie stepped into the fading daylight. Jack stepped out after her.

The sun had gone down.

They were standing *outside* the gate of the Dragon King's palace. They could see the market not far away. The stalls were closing for the day.

"We're safe!" said Annie.

Jack breathed a huge sigh of relief.

Just then, a gong sounded. It was coming

from the tower of the city walls!

"Oh, man! They're going to close the gates!" said Jack.

He clutched his sack as they took off. They charged up the street. They ran past the market. They ran past the rich houses...past the poor houses.

Their straw shoes fell off. But Jack and Annie kept running barefoot.

Just as the giant wooden gates started to close, they tore through them.

They charged across the bridge and kept running up the dirt road, past the farmhouse, and through the field.

By the time they reached their tree, Jack's lungs ached. His heart pounded. His feet burned.

He followed Annie up the rope ladder. When they got inside the tree house, Jack collapsed.

"Let's—go—home," he said, out of breath.

He reached for the Pennsylvania book.

"Wait," said Annie, looking out the window. "They found each other."

"Who—found—who?" said Jack, panting.

He dragged himself to the window and looked out.

Two figures embraced at the edge of the field.

"The silk weaver and the man who takes care of the cows!" said Annie.

"Oh, yeah," said Jack.

"Bye!" Annie called to them.

The couple waved back.

Annie sighed happily.

"We can leave now," she said.

Jack opened the Pennsylvania book and pointed at the picture of the Frog Creek woods.

"I wish we could go there," he said.

The wind started to blow.

Jack looked out one last time at the Chinese couple. They seemed to be glowing like stars.

The tree house started to spin.

It spun faster and faster.

Then everything was still.

Absolutely still.

10

The Ancient Legend

Jack opened his eyes. He was wearing his own clothes and his sneakers. The cloth sack had turned back into his backpack.

"Welcome home, Master Librarians," said Morgan.

She stood in the tree house, smiling at them.

"Hi!" said Annie.

"We brought you the ancient legend," said Jack.

"Wonderful!" said Morgan.

Jack reached into his pack. He took out the China book. Then he pulled out the bamboo book. He handed them to Morgan.

"What's the legend about?" said Annie.

"It's called *The Silk Weaver and the Cowherd*," said Morgan. "It's a very famous Chinese tale."

"Guess what, Morgan?" said Annie. "We actually *met* them! We helped them get together!"

"Oh, did you?" said Morgan.

"Yes!" said Jack. "The silk weaver's ball of silk saved us!"

"What does the legend say about them?" asked Annie.

"It says that long ago they were heavenly beings who lived in the sky," said Morgan.

"When they came to earth, they fell in love."

"That's when we met them!" said Annie.

"Yes, I imagine so," said Morgan. "The book you brought back tells about their happiness on earth. But I'm afraid a later legend tells us that when they returned to the sky, the king and queen of the skies separated them by a heavenly river called the Milky Way."

"Oh, no," said Annie.

"They get back together once a year," said Morgan. "On that night, birds make a bridge in the sky over the Milky Way."

Jack and Annie gazed up at the bright summer sky.

"Go home now," said Morgan. "Come back two weeks from today. Next you're going to find a book in the country of Ireland, over a thousand years ago."

"That sounds like fun," said Annie.

Morgan frowned.

"I'm afraid it was a very dangerous time," she said. "For Viking raiders often attacked the seacoasts."

"Vikings?" said Jack. He'd had enough danger to last a long time.

"Don't worry about it now," said Morgan. "Just go home and rest."

Jack nodded.

"I'll try," he said, pulling on his backpack.

"Bye," said Annie. "See you in two weeks."

"Thank you for your help," said Morgan.

"Anytime," said Annie.

They headed down the rope ladder.

From the ground, they waved to Morgan. Then they started for home.

As they got to the edge of the woods, Annie stopped.

"Listen to the crickets," she said.

Jack listened. The cricket chirps sounded louder than usual.

"Their ancestors lived in the time of the Dragon King," said Annie.

"Oh, brother," said Jack.

"Right now the grownups are telling the little crickets a legend," said Annie.

"Yeah, sure," said Jack.

"A legend passed down from their ancestors," said Annie.

Jack smiled. He didn't want to admit it, but the cricket noise *did* sound like storytelling. He could almost hear them saying, *Dragon King, Dragon King, Dragon King.*

"Jack! Annie!" came a voice.

It was their mother calling them.

The spell was broken. The cricket stories were just plain old cricket sounds again.

"Coming!" Jack shouted.

Jack and Annie ran down their street and across their yard.

"Did you have a good time in China?" their mom asked.

"It was pretty scary," said Annie.

"We got lost in a tomb," said Jack. "But we were saved by an ancient book."

Their mom smiled and shook her head. "My, books are wonderful, aren't they?" she said.

"Yep!" said Jack and Annie.

And they followed her inside.

Don't miss the next Magic Tree House book,
when Jack and Annie are whisked back to
ancient Ireland to find another book in

MAGIC TREE HOUSE #15

VIKING SHIPS
AT SUNRISE

(August 1998)

Where have *you* traveled in the

The Mystery of the Tree House
(Books #1–4)

☐ **Magic Tree House #1, Dinosaurs Before Dark,** in which Jack and Annie discover the tree house and travel back to the time of dinosaurs.

☐ **Magic Tree House #2, The Knight at Dawn,** in which Jack and Annie go to the time of knights and explore a medieval castle with a hidden passage.

☐ **Magic Tree House #3, Mummies in the Morning,** in which Jack and Annie go to ancient Egypt and get lost in a pyramid when they help a ghost queen.

☐ **Magic Tree House #4, Pirates Past Noon,** in which Jack and Annie travel back in time and meet some unfriendly pirates searching for buried treasure.

The Mystery of the Magic Spell
(Books #5–8)

❑ **Magic Tree House #5, Night of the Ninjas,** in which Jack and Annie go to old Japan and learn the secrets of the ninjas.

❑ **Magic Tree House #6, Afternoon on the Amazon,** in which Jack and Annie explore the wild rain forest of the Amazon and are greeted by giant ants, hungry crocodiles, and flesh-eating piranhas.

❑ **Magic Tree House #7, Sunset of the Sabertooth,** in which Jack and Annie go back to the Ice Age—the world of woolly mammoths, sabertooth tigers, and a mysterious sorcerer.

❑ **Magic Tree House #8, Midnight on the Moon,** in which Jack and Annie go forward in time to a space station on the moon, where they ride in a moon buggy and have a close encounter with a moon man.

The Mystery of the Ancient Riddles
(Books #9–12)

❏ **Magic Tree House #9, Dolphins at Daybreak,** in which Jack and Annie arrive on a coral reef, where they find a mini-submarine that takes them underwater into the home of sharks and dolphins.

❏ **Magic Tree House #10, Ghost Town at Sundown,** in which Jack and Annie travel to the Wild West, where they battle horse thieves, meet a kindly cowboy, and get some help from a mysterious ghost.

❏ **Magic Tree House #11, Lions at Lunchtime,** in which Jack and Annie go to the plains of Africa, where they help wild animals cross a rushing river and have a picnic with a Masai warrior.

❏ **Magic Tree House #12, Polar Bears Past Bedtime,** in which Jack and Annie go to the Arctic, where they get help from a seal hunter, play with polar bear cubs, and get trapped on thin ice.

The Mystery of the Lost Libraries
(Books #13–16)

☐ **Magic Tree House #13, VACATION UNDER THE VOLCANO,** in which Jack and Annie land in Pompeii during Roman times, on the very day that Mount Vesuvius erupts.

Read all the Magic Tree House books!

Available wherever books are sold...OR
You can send in this coupon (with check or money order)
and have the books mailed directly to you!

❑ Magic Tree House #1, DINOSAURS BEFORE DARK
(0-679-82411-1) $3.99

❑ Magic Tree House #2, THE KNIGHT AT DAWN
(0-679-82412-X) $3.99

❑ Magic Tree House #3, MUMMIES IN THE MORNING
(0-679-82424-3) $3.99

❑ Magic Tree House #4, PIRATES PAST NOON
(0-679-82425-1) $3.99

❑ Magic Tree House #5, NIGHT OF THE NINJAS
(0-679-86371-0) $3.99

❑ Magic Tree House #6, AFTERNOON ON THE AMAZON
(0-679-86372-9) $3.99

❑ Magic Tree House #7, SUNSET OF THE SABERTOOTH
(0-679-86373-7) $3.99

❑ Magic Tree House #8, MIDNIGHT ON THE MOON
(0-679-86374-5) $3.99

❑ Magic Tree House #9, DOLPHINS AT DAYBREAK
(0-679-88338-X) $3.99

❑ Magic Tree House #10, GHOST TOWN AT SUNDOWN
(0-679-88339-8) $3.99

❑ Magic Tree House #11, LIONS AT LUNCHTIME
(0-679-88340-1) $3.99

❑ Magic Tree House #12, POLAR BEARS PAST BEDTIME
(0-679-88341-X) $3.99

❑ Magic Tree House #13, VACATION UNDER THE VOLCANO
(0-679-89050-5) $3.99

Subtotal ....$ _____
Shipping and handling............................$ __3.00__
Sales tax (where applicable)............... _____
Total amount enclosed............................$ _____

Name _____

Address _____

City _____ State _____ Zip _____

Prices and numbers subject to change without notice. Valid in U.S. only.
All orders subject to availability. Please allow 4 to 6 weeks for delivery.

Make your check or money order (no cash or C.O.D.s)
payable to Random House, Inc., and mail to:
Magic Tree House Mail Sales, 400 Hahn Road, Westminster, MD 21157.

Need your books even faster? Call toll-free 1-800-793-2665
to order by phone and use your major credit card

MORE FACTS FOR YOU AND JACK

1. Chinese writing has over 50,000 characters. According to legend, the first characters were devised from the tracks of birds and animals.

2. In 221 B.C., China was divided into many kingdoms. Under the leadership of the first emperor, Shi Huangdi (who called himself the Dragon King), China became a united country. Afraid that Chinese scholars were a threat to his power, he ordered all their books burned.

3. Silk thread comes from the cocoon of the silkworm, which feeds on mulberry leaves. The art of making silk was kept a secret because the Chinese once depended on silk for foreign trade.

4. The first emperor built the Great Wall to protect his empire from northern invaders. According to Chinese legend, the wall is a dragon that has turned to stone.

5. Since the 1970s, archaeologists have been investigating the Dragon King's tomb and have unearthed over 50,000 artifacts.

6. The Chinese legend of the silk weaver and the cowherd is connected with the stars Vega and Altair. The two were married on earth. But when they returned to heaven, they were so happy that they refused to work. The king and queen of Heaven grew angry and separated them by the Milky Way. But once a year, they are together. On the seventh day of the seventh moon, magpies make a bridge between them.

Look for these other Random House books
by Mary Pope Osborne!

Picture books:

Molly and the Prince
Moonhorse

For middle-grade readers:

American Tall Tales
One World, Many Religions

And available in 1999,
the Spider Kane mysteries!

*Spider Kane and the Mystery Under
    the May-Apple (#1)*
*Spider Kane and the Mystery at
    Jumbo Nightcrawler's (#2)*

The *New York Times* Bestselling Series!

Battle a Blizzard with Jack and Annie!

MAGIC TREE HOUSE #36
A MERLIN MISSION

Blizzard of the **Blue Moon**

Mary Pope Osborne

Merlin has asked Jack and Annie to help on another magical mission! This time they travel back in time to New York City during the great Depression. In the midst of a terrible snowstorm, Jack and Annie must save a unicorn. But where are they going to find a unicorn in a big city? And who are the mysterious people following them?

Look for these MERLIN MISSIONS titles wherever books are sold.

Visit www.magictreehouse.com for games and activities!

RHCB

244

MAGIC  TREE HOUSE®

Ooh la la

Save the day with Jack and Annie

Merlin sends Jack and Annie on a magical adventure to the 1889 World's Fair in Paris, France. There they must save four new magicians from an evil sorcerer!

Illustrations © 2006 by Sal Murdocca.

The *New York Times* Bestselling Series!

Look for these MERLIN MISSION titles wherever books are sold.

 RANDOM HOUSE CHILDREN'S BOOKS   LISTENING LIBRARY

www.magictreehouse.com